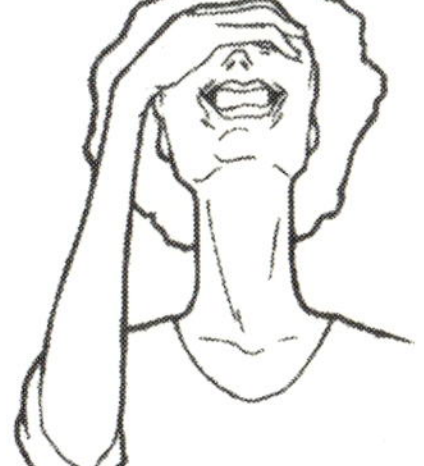

LAUGH LINES

AND OTHER WRINKLES

Poems by

Chris Oosterbaan
and
Joyce Snow

Illustrations by

Brian Carey

C& J Lines
Richland, Michigan

Cover art and all illustrations in the book
are by Brian Carey.

Authors photograph by Terri Cooper

C& J Lines
Richland, Michigan

Laugh Lines and Other Wrinkles

ISBN 978-1-938911-27-9

Design and typesetting
Ann Paulson, Paulson Communications

First Printing, 2012
Fidlar Doubleday, Davenport, Iowa

TO

Women everywhere
young, old and older.

DEDICATED

To our two favorite Edies,
our mothers,
Edith Cooper and Edith Probasco.
who aged graciously,
sharing their wit
and wisdom through the years.

LAUGH LINES

AND OTHER WRINKLES

LAUGH LINES

THE HEALTH CLUB

One day feeling frisky,
I did something risky
And off to the health club I went.

If I could reduce,
If my pants could be loose,
That would be money well spent.

First there was spinning
Right from the beginning
I knew it wasn't my style.

They were all dripping sweat
Their hair, soaking wet
I never saw one of them smile!

The Yoga teacher said, "Hi,
Come give it a try."
She had me get down on the floor.

It wasn't so pretty
When it took a committee
To render me upright once more!

I checked out Pilates
Those pretzel thin bodies
I tried just one move and said, "Nix!"

As the old saying goes
And most everyone knows
You can't teach an old dog new tricks.

Then, while we were talking
Some guy said, "Try walking.
It's great. You don't have to go far."

He seemed really nice
So I took his advice
And I walked out the door to my car!

ORGANS

Ashes to ashes, dust to dust
Not an organ left working
A poor girl can trust

BLADDER

Bladder, bladder, gone astray
Let me down another day
Just when I think I'm dry and safe
I've dribbled and begun to chafe

SURGERY

My doctor has advised a hysterectomy
Why can't he fix my wrinkled neck
  and replace my knee?
Add to that my bunion
  and pop-up hammer toe
I've given him the green light
  and said, "Doc, have a go!"

My warranty's expired on several body parts
so why can't he, to humor me,
  just finish what he starts?!

BEAUTY SECRETS

One erases dark spots
One helps wrinkles puff
One will firm the neck and chin
One makes dead skin slough
Dab one on the lips,
And one around the eyes
Maybe try the kind
Oprah Winfrey buys!

Night cream, day cream
All so confusing . . .
How does my skin know
Which one I'm using?

CALENDAR GIRL

My calendar is oh, so full
I'm busy every minute
Frankly, not a day goes by
Without a doctor in it

Monday it's my EKG
Tuesday it's my shrink
Wednesday I see my Internist
He'll say I'm in the pink

Thursday someone checks my teeth
Removing all the plaque
Friday I squeeze in my mammogram
I swear I'll not go back

Then it's time for lab work
The nurse will draw some blood
She'll make me pee into a cup
I hope it doesn't flood

These appointments are annoying
They cause me grief and strife
But if they all got cancelled
I'd have no social life

GRAY MATTER

To dye or not to dye? That is the question
  to ask when your hair's turning gray
Whether 'tis nobler to halt the advancement
or to let Father Time have his way.

Women have discovered that
  though gray is covered,
it won't go away. It keeps living.
You never know when, but again and again
gray is the gift that keeps giving.

NAME THAT TUNE

Wrinkle, wrinkle, little face
How I wonder what took place

Up above my neck so high
Little lines so deep and dry

Wrinkle, wrinkle, little face
How I wonder what took place!

UPGRADES

The younger folks get facelifts
Smoother skin and fuller lips
My friends spend their money
On shoulders, knees and hips

While the youthful set looks classy
As they run or smile or talk
You can bet our older set
Is thankful just to walk

CHANGING FACE

A face can change in forty years
Mapped by smiles, etched by tears
Ah, you ask me how I know
My trusty mirror tells me so

SPLITTING HAIRS

My hairs have been splitting
So brutally shed
Clumped on my hair brush
Instead of my head

No shaving or plucking
Hairs surprisingly sparse
Now shaving my legs
Is somewhat of a farce

SUITED UP

I tug, I pull
I yank, I squeeze
Finally I'm in!
Behold my rippled thighs
  and knees,
Behold my pasty skin
I check out my reflection
. . .It's anything but cute
I may regret it,
but give me credit.
I'm in my bathing suit!

NEW DIET

New diet?
I'll try it
tomorrow, I vow.
To my sorrow
I'll just eat my words
(plus the chow).

SALT & PEPPER ARMS

My friends and I still seem to think
we're full of girlish charms
But as we've aged, we look askance
at "salt and pepper" arms

We smile and wave at good old friends
and some we hope to make
Too late we see that loose arm flesh
shake and shake and shake

OLD FRIENDS LOST

What happened to my old friends?
They don't know left from right
Lost their hearing, sense of smell
Good balance and their sight

Lost their nerve and cheerfulness
Good looks and memories
Waistlines spread and so did hips
Boobs fell to their knees

What happened to my old friends?
Is very strange to tell
I hardly recognize them now
They haven't aged too well

CLOSET CASE

Sometimes when I'm in the kitchen
stirring soup or secretly snacking,
I dream of how pretty I'd be
if my wardrobe were not sadly lacking.

I'd pull out my basic black dress
With pearls I'd look classy and slim
or my cute sassy shorts and a tank top
in case I went off to the gym.

I'd wear silks and softest cashmere,
belts and scarves to accessorize,
I'd be preening in pants and jeans
that don't adhere to my thighs.

I'd be proud of my lingerie,
My bras would be truly uplifting,
designed for someone substantial
whose topography seems to be shifting.

But, it's clear as I look in the mirror
before leaving my dressing room,
No matter how much I buy or how hard I try,
I'll never be Heidi Klum!

REAR VIEW

When people see me coming,
I think I look okay
But when they see me going,
I wonder what they say

Do the neighbors gawk and giggle
When I bring in the mail
Whispering behind my back,
"Now, that's an old wife's tail!"

THE TERRIBLE FIGHT

I had a terrible fight today.
I thought she was my friend.
Pals together through thick and thin
Now our partnership must end.

I had valued her opinion.
Truth was always on her side.
Now she simply sat there
As I watched a frightening slide.

Our fight turned nasty fast
And it really made no sense.
I feared it might get rough
My wrath was so intense.

I said, "On guard, you demon.
You should be so ashamed.
You haven't got *a snowball's chance*
In Hell to win this game."

I could have chosen to ignore her
To cheat and look away.
I could accept this one transgression
And go merrily on my way.

But, stumbling from the bathroom
I left a tearful trail.
I knew I'd lost the battle
To my nemesis, the scale.

FACE IN THE MIRROR

I looked into the mirror
And glaring back I see
An old decrepit hag
Was that really me?

What happened to that neck?
It's full of crepey skin
I want to put some makeup on
But fear it will sink in.

Those eyes have added circles
The cheeks have headed south
I see dingy, yellow teeth
Inside a worn out mouth.

The tortured hair's a mess
The hair that's left, that is
Clinging so relentlessly
Reduced to stringy frizz.

Those wrinkles, crinkles, dark spots
What a sight to see
The reflection, although fuzzy
Shows a sad finality.

I'd put my glasses on and yet
If this image gets much clearer
I'll be forced to vent my rage
And break this useless mirror.

CLASSIFIED AD

For Sale: A wedding dress
Worn once years ago
With tiara and veil
That I choose to let go

Not sure of the size
Perhaps it's a ten
Can't wear it or bear
To see it again

The groom broke our vows
Moved on with his life
Found a new job and family
And much younger wife

The dress still has beauty
Though life let me down
The promise remains
In this long satin gown

Come see for yourself
A bargain indeed
This used wedding dress
Is just what you need

THROUGH THICK AND THIN

Those old family photos don't lie
They show what great shape I was in
Years ago my hair was much thicker
And my body, surprisingly thin.

Funny how things have reversed
I'm thick where I don't want to be,
Shaped like a pear, topped by thin hair,
Yet through thick and thin I'm still me.

TRUISM

"What goes around comes around"
   was true when I was svelte
I don't believe it anymore
   and neither does my belt.

THE BATHTUB

The bathtub is so alluring
I'd really love to get in
Lie back in the frothy bubbles
Hot water up to my chin

It's not that I don't have the time
It's simply that shadow of doubt
I can enter the water with ease
But my knees might not let me out!

HALLOWEEN

I bought the candy early
  It's on my secret shelf
Just a little trick of mine
  So I can treat myself.

LOVE AND MARRIAGE

The thrill of the hunt
The spectacular chase
It all happened lightning fast

A flowery wedding
With warm heartfelt vows
Let this be a marriage to last

True love and devotion
We're pledging today
With toasts and best wishes galore

Free flowing champagne
And friends' fingers crossed
Wish me luck, I'm wife number four

HEALTH ADVICE

She died at 96
She had an iron will
She didn't believe in doctors
She never took a pill

"Stay away from doctors!"
That was her dance and song
"If they poke you long enough,
They'll find something wrong!"

UNFAITHFUL MAN:
A CAUTIONARY TALE

It seemed so simple
Faith—that is
Vows were spoken
Mine and his

Mid-life crisis
Spawned a thought
He planned to cheat
And not get caught

He wandered off
With a younger honey
Left with naught,
I took his money

Now he's alone
Young honey fled
His spirit's battered
His face is red

While I survived
Flourished fine
Grew rather rich
My life sublime

The cheating man
Must pay a price
For faith thus scorned
A wicked vice

So, men be true
To your dear wife
Or face alone
A dismal life

JOINTLY SPEAKING

Getting up is a joint effort
I stand for a moment to see
if my hips will give me the slip
or if I can count on my knee

I turn my head, left to right
and listen intently to check
for the snap, crackle and pop
that emanate from my neck

I stretch one arm toward the ceiling
feeling a stab in my shoulder. . .
I think my joints have made their point—
No bones about it—I'm older!

BLUE WINE

I wish there were a blue wine
Though it sounds quite idiotic
Sipping on my nightly wine
I'd feel so patriotic

White wine with hors d'oeuvres
Red wine served with dinner
Blue wine with a sweet dessert
I'd have a three-course winner

There'd be no stopping me
I could drink all night that way
Each glass consumed with glory
To salute the USA

MONEY TALK

He: My dear, let's have a little chat
about the family budget.

She: By now I thought that you'd know how
to make ends meet or fudge it.

He: You've got to balance the checkbook.
Won't you just try it, honey?

She: Well, if I do, I'm warning you,
you'll find we're out of money!

MOTHER-IN-LAW

It seems she can only see him
as her pride and joy
Not a man with a wife and a grownup life,
No longer her dear little boy.

Such a mother-in-law can be sticky
(Though ***he*** may find her endearing)
She pretends to take a back seat,
when, in fact, she's apt to be steering.

She calls at inopportune times,
She stops in at the drop of a hat,
She takes your sweet child for a week
and returns him —a spoiled brat.

She tastes your entrée with a smile,
a smile that says, "You poor dear,
how do you keep from starving?"
Her unspoken message is clear.

You hate unwrapping her presents
and putting them on display.
You think—heck, why can't she give me a check
since she knows there are bills to pay?

She appears to inspect your home,
eyes darting from ceiling to floor
Then she whispers to your husband
when he walks her out to the door.

Just keep track of all her tricks,
how she jockeys to stay number one. . .
For you'll be taking those reins one day
when someone marries your son!

COLLEGE REUNION

My reunion's coming up real soon
And I have lots to do
  Lift my face
  Trim my waist
And shed a pound or two

My wardrobe needs updating
My closet sings the blues
  Need to shop
  'Til I drop
For outfits and new shoes

Yes, it's a big reunion
We'll laugh and shed some tears
  As we embrace
  Each new face
And ponder 50 years

I'm looking forward to the party
Those friendships made of gold
  What a surprise
  To recognize
That we've all grown mighty old

MY GRANDSON

Gazing at my grandson
I think he couldn't be cuter
sitting like a businessman
in front of the computer

I watch him boot it up
He enters some cool game
I thought we might play checkers
He thought that would be lame

To regain his attention
I try my grandma tricks
cookies? candy? ice cream?
Good grief, he's only six!

SINGLE AT 70

I used to ogle younger men
Handsome and well-muscled
Run my fingers through their hair
'Til it was roughly tussled

Now I'm fond of thinning hair
A pot belly to boot
My dates can look like anything
As long as they have loot

WELCOME HOME, DEAR

The casserole burned to a crisp,
I've lost my credit card,
The toilet's making gurgling sounds,
Moles have invaded the yard,

Gas prices are up again,
The market's heading down,
The dentist checked my throbbing tooth
He said I'd need a crown,

I tried to clean your favorite shirt
With Clorox and with Shout—
It turned a different color,
But the spot did not come out

Aunt Fran has planned a visit
Guess where she wants to stay?
Enough about me —What about you,
Darling? How was your day?

MEMOIR OF A HOSTESS

Long ago I had dinner parties
I'd polish the silverware,
clean the house, top to bottom
'til it looked like no one lived there
I'd plan a gourmet menu,
fret over dishes for hours,
ship the kids off to Grandma's,
and dress up the table with flowers
We'd party long after midnight
then there were dishes to do
I'd put everything back in order
and fall into bed at two

I marvel at how I did it,
all that work, those late nights way back when. . .
Now I just make reservations
and we're home and in bed by ten.

NOT A CADILLAC

My little grandsons heard me talking
How naive and sweet they are
When I said I have a cataract,
They thought I'd bought a car!

FUGITIVE

Granny and her motor chair
    have taken to the road
She's left the dratted nursing home for good
Her escape has gone unnoticed
    so she thinks she won't be missed
And that she'll settle in some pleasant
    neighborhood

When granny packed her suitcase
    and put her clothes inside
She didn't take much notice of her stuff
She left nothing out to wear
    and doesn't seem to care
That she's driving down the sidewalk in the buff.

FOOTBALL MOM

Praise for the football mom
Who never does complain
Who nightly washes uniforms
Sits Fridays in the rain

Praise her for healthy dinners
For spraying his shoes for the stench
For cheering and silently wishing
Her son could get off the bench

HIS OTHER LOVER

My husband has taken a lover
She sits faithfully by his side
She pushes his buttons when he pushes hers
Like a smitten honeymoon bride

He woos her, he courts her, he holds her
Even thieves couldn't be thicker
He leaves her only when he's off to sleep
His mistress, the TV clicker

WRITER'S EXCUSES

I chose today, set it aside
I'd write my poem first
Nothing would deter me
Except maybe a hearse

I pulled my chair up to my desk
Ah me, the loyal bard
I waited for my brain to work
Increasingly, that's hard

Writing was my goal today
A poem is a must
Waiting for a rhyme or theme
I noticed all the dust

I've never been a tidy soul
But cleaning is a breeze
Much easier than writing
When rhymes don't flow with ease

I picked the litter off the floor
And got the vacuum out
How could I be creative
With such filth and grime about

So now my place is spotless
My desk now spic and span
I'll face my desk and blank PC
To write —yes, that's my plan

WEDDING GUESTS

I.
They sit through the ceremony,
wives dabbing tears from their eyes
The husbands fidget and fumble,
attempting to loosen their ties
The women pay rapt attention
to the bride, to her gown, to her veil
The men sympathize with the groom
who looks rather sickly and pale

II.
Arriving at the reception
the wives admire the flowers
The husbands keep checking their watches,
wondering how many more hours
Hot hors d'oeuvres come on silver trays
The wives sample one, maybe two
Off to the bar go the men
to huddle and belt down a few

III.
It's time to be seated for dinner
The women are signaling the men
who seat their wives with a flourish
and head to the bar once again
Laughing, the wives clink their glasses
to elicit a newlywed kiss
Meanwhile the men are checking the score
of the game they were forced to miss

IV.
The band has begun to play
The music is youthful and loud
The wives would love to get out there
but what if their partners are plowed?
Finally the cake has been cut
The wives savor every sweet bite
They see their men sipping cognac
It's time to call it a night!

V.
Weary wives march off to their cars
They have the keys and they're mad
The husbands plop in beside them,
mumbling what a great time they had.
Back home husbands stumble to bed
It's over, the night they were dreading
While the wives are convincing themselves
There's nothing more fun than a wedding!

THE HOLIDAYS

It's Xmas time, hurry scurry
Spending money —what a worry

Host the family, cook the food
Slap Aunt Alice when she's rude

Send the cards, clean the place
Party with a smiling face

Buy the presents, trim the tree
Stressing out, no time for me

Xmas time, it gives me pause
I feel as old as Mrs. Claus

Fragile nerves, I'm on the brink
The Holidays —so glad I drink!

A MOTHER'S LAMENT

My oldest son is aging
Soon he'll mark another year
Sometimes my reflections
Bring a lonesome tear

I still want to protect him
I hope it's not too late
Tomorrow is his birthday
He's turning 48

PARTY TIME

Primaries, polls and pundits
It's dog eat dog again
Paid promises and platforms
and we don't vote 'til when?

To fetch the nomination
they'll do most anything
Like a pack of wild dogs
they dig up mud to sling

One snarls through the fray
the others come up short
They heel and lick their wounds
proclaiming full support

The Convention comes at last
Top Dog will speak and win
For now he's Best in Show. . .
  Let the Big Dog Race begin!

REFLECTIONS ON LAKE MICHIGAN

I.
A billion trillion grains of sand
Make up the beach, 'tis said
Tonight it feels like all of them
Got made up in my bed

II.
Scientists claim the earth is round
I can't imagine that
Pondering the endless lake
I'd swear the earth was flat

FLORIDA

"Florida is so boring,"
That's what young people say
"It's where the old folks go."
Guess what —–I'm on my way!

GAY PAREE

I'd like to pack up my valise
and spend a month in France
Gay Paree, that's where I'd be
were I to have *la chance.*

You'd find me sipping coffee
at an intimate café
nibbling cheese and warm croissants
along the Champs Èlysées.

I'd meet the Mona Lisa
and stare at her a while
perhaps unlock the mystery
of her enigmatic smile.

Atop the Eiffel Tower
I'd wear a black béret
"*Quel dommage,*"is what I'd say
as it blew away.

Nôtre Dame and Sacre Coeur
a boat ride on the Seine
Some escargots! Why can't I go?
I ask him once again.

Ooh, là, là, so much I'd do
and oh how much I'd see
if only Monsieur Moneybags
would learn to say,"*Oui, oui!*"

GLOBAL WARNING

Here I am once more,
turning up the thermostat
I'd like to meet Al Gore
and sit down for a chat

I'd say, "Look out there, Al
Another winter storm!
Here's the inconvenient truth:
It really isn't warm!"

JANET JACKSON

Janet's wardrobe malfunction
created a national stir
Guys who keep abreast of the news
all really felt for her

TWEETING AND TWITTERING

Tweeting and twittering, that's for the birds
Facebook is missing my face,
Texting and sexting to me are perplexing,
I guess I'm an archaic case

I'm not so accessible, but I'm addressable
By letter or by phone
I don't give a tweet that I'm obsolete
Technology, leave me alone!

ISABELLE PUCK

Did you hear what happened to Isabelle Puck?
She got run over by a garbage truck
They put her together with glue and paste
She died anyway —what a waste

GUESSING GAME

One day when I was shopping
And feeling rather bold,
Convinced I looked quite stylish,
Mature but not too old
I asked a cute, young salesclerk
To try to guess my age
Her sky high number left me
In a fit of elder rage

I swung my purse and missed her
I swung it once again
Luckily she ducked the blows
I must admit since then
I've been feeling rather foolish
And I've hated feeling older
While nursing my bruised ego
. . .and my dislocated shoulder

HIGHLY RECOMMENDED

I say to those people out there
who think they really don't need them,
Just look how light weight they are
It doesn't take much to feed them

They'll improve your disposition
They do wonders for your heart
You can teach them all kinds of tricks
You'll find them adorably smart

If you think they sound intriguing
If you think you'd like to try one
Put in a request to those you love best
in hopes they will supply one

They take several months to deliver
but what a grand day it will be
when your daughter or son presents you with one
You'll be ecstatic, trust me!

AND OTHER WRINKLES

ELDER CINDERELLA

An elder Cinderella
   thinks she's going to the ball
Awaiting her, Prince Charming
   is in the dining hall
No slippers made of fragile glass
   adorn her weathered feet
Her slippers, thick and woolen,
   hold in the summer's heat

No pumpkin is her carriage,
   no horses morphed from mice
She's lucky to have lived so long
   but she has paid a price
She rouges up her cheeks,
   stuffs hankies in her sleeves
She hopes to reach the dining hall
   before Prince Charming leaves

Her ball gown is a faded robe,
   no jewelry does she wear
No step-sisters surround her,
   just aides who truly care
She moves on wings of memories,
   the wheelchair glides along
There is no music playing
   yet her heart is filled with song

The dining hall has emptied,
   but her prince is waiting there
Just as she imagined him,
   sitting in his chair
They wheel her to his table,
   she listens for the band
The prince arises gallantly,
   extends a shaky hand

He bends to push her slippers on
   with a tender touch
Cinderella smiles at him,
   remembering so much
They cling to dreams of dancing,
   on feet once feather light
And hope they'll meet to dance again,
   perhaps tomorrow night

ALZHEIMER'S

He took her ring for safekeeping
she looked up like a frightened child
"It's just for a while," he promised
he touched her face and she smiled

She had never taken it off
not once in fifty-three years
so many broken promises
he wondered if she saw his tears

HOLDING ON

A strange wind swept through
when my father died
washing memories
like shells on welcome sand
hundreds of them

Too many to collect at once
they wait for me
scattered across the days to come
when time and again
I'll return to the water's edge

LETTER TO A FRIEND

If I could ease your troubles
Here is what I'd do
Circle you within my arms
Speak words to comfort you

I'd wave a wand and wish away
The past few painful years
And get a soft, new handkerchief
To dry up all those tears

I'd conjure up some magic
To brighten up your spacc
Dance or sing or tell a joke
Put smiles upon your face

I'd make a pill or tonic
To calm your anguished mind
I'd search for unique presents
And give you what I find

Since I can't ease the pain
My power is oh, so slight
I'll keep you in my fondest thoughts
And pray with all my might

FUNERAL

I sit with memories today
I've lost another friend
finality reminding me
of fences I must mend
of bitter weeds I must pull
to let the roses climb
to see them dance on stems of thorns,
perennial as time.

VISITATION

No choice but to face it
she gathers up her grief
the widow wearing black,
she stands in unbelief

Grasping sympathetic hands
she trembles through the hours
while he—how could he leave her?
—sleeps among the flowers.

WHY?

He left life in a hurry
packed up all the answers
and moved into the night

Even in morning sunlight
we were blinded

TOM

Booming voice,
hearty laugh
Silenced now.

Sparkling blue eyes,
closed forever
Heaven bound.

FEBRUARY

Onions purr in hot butter. I'm making soup
  because Sandy has cancer

She and I used to wonder what kind of men
  our sons would be

I think of Sandy unfolding memories
  holding them to her cheek like old laces

Now the heavy tomatoes seep red into the broth
  three handfuls of rice begin to swell

I'm making soup for Sandy because
  this is a recipe that always turns out

TO EMILY DICKINSON

She never saw a moor
She never saw the sea
Yet what a brilliant mind she had
To know what those would be

She never spoke with God
Nor had she been to heaven
Yet she had faith as once I had
When I was six or seven

TURNING 70

Looking back I see so clearly
things I should have nixed,
things that needed fixing,
things I should have fixed

Looking back I see some people
who deserved the best of me
Those people in my busyness
only got the rest of me

I've worn the hats life gave me
daughter, mother, wife and friend,
hats I wore quite nicely,
hats I've had to mend

There are dreams I chased and lost,
regrets that followed me
My glass, half empty is half full
I'm where I ought to be

Ups and downs, I've known my share
through three score years and ten
Had I the chance, I'd look askance
at living them again!

THE LETTER

We never talk of war. Never.
But at least I still have the letter, saved deep in a bureau drawer. It was written by my brother in September 1966 —mailed from Vietnam.

I was oblivious to the war. I was married.
My little boy had just turned two
and I was bulging with another pregnancy
—due in 10 weeks.

My brother was a Forward Observer in Vietnam,
first to spot the enemy on the front line.
I read his letter for the hundredth time.

> *Hi Sis,*
>
> *Hope all is well there. I am fine.*
>
> *Once in a while I step over dead bodies. They are so young. I try not to look down at their faces.*
>
> *It's so hot over here.*
>
> *I predict you will have a baby girl on December 6.*
>
> *I miss you all.*

I had only seen photos of the hippy protesters booing and throwing things at returning soldiers, only seen photos of Jane Fonda. I did not understand. I did not have time to understand.

I was busy deciding if my son was ready for a big bed or old enough to be potty trained. I was busy getting a new crib ready.

My son is now 48. The baby girl, born on December 5, is 46. My brother is 69, married with adult children of his own.

Vietnam is a closed chapter.

GRANDPA'S KNEE

I still remember Grandpa's knee
A place secure as it could be
On his lap and in his chair
So much of life I learned right there

It really didn't matter much
If he gave a tender touch
Or if he read or sang or sat
Or rocked or took the time to chat

I often feel a need to share
The peacefulness of sitting there
Whatever age I grow to be
I'll feel the love from Grandpa's knee

OLD LADY

I met someone old today
I looked at her and cried
Her skin was pale and wrinkled
Her hair was clearly dyed

The lady's youth had vanished
She looked through cloudy eyes
Her back was slightly hunched
She'd shrunk to half her size

There was no conversation
But we connected in a way
We formed a bond, for we both knew
We'd meet again one day

As she slowly wandered off
We could silently agree
Though it was left unspoken
That old lady would be me

COFFEE KLATCH

Drinking my coffee with gossip
pretending I agree . . .
I think I'm forgetting too often
who I started out to be.

SIXTEEN

This week he turned sixteen
and he just can't understand
why so reluctantly I place
the car keys in his hand
I blow a kiss and whisper
as he drives out of sight,
"Please, Guardian Angels, please,
stay with my boy tonight."

HER VOICE

Hers was the voice calling us home
from the hilly orchard
where we hurled soft apples
and hid among the lacy trees

Hers was the voice calling us home
from the farm across Oakland Drive
where we ran along the wire fence
shadowing the old horse,
reaching in to know his soft breath

Hers was the voice calling us home
from the stream behind our house
where we stood, knee-deep, hunting frogs
screaming when we found bloodsuckers
slimy black on our feet

Hers was the voice calling us home
from the dark floating time
before we even knew ourselves,
through sunlit childhood and
all the years beyond

Hers was the voice calling us home

LIFE'S PATH

Life is a path through the woods
You must carefully make your own way
Choosing which path to follow
Is the serious game we all play.

One day go left, next day go right
You'll be forced to finally decide
It's all up to you but when you feel blue
There'll be some path you'll wish you had tried.

That place in between, while safe as can be
Is no help in solving the riddle
If you don't use your voice
   and make a clear choice
You'll stay caught in the troublesome middle.

GRANDEST MOMENT

There's a singular moment in life
   more shining, more precious than gold
when your heart and your arms open wide
   and you have a grandchild to hold

POEMS BY CHRIS OOSTERBAAN

The Health Club
Surgery
Beauty Secrets
Gray Matter
Name That Tune
Suited Up
New Diet
Closet Case
Rear View
Through Thick and Thin
Truism
The Bath Tub
Halloween
Health Advice
Jointly Speaking
Money Talk
Mother-in-Law
My Grandson
Welcome Home, Dear
Memoir of a Hostess
Not a Cadillac
Wedding Guests
Party Time
Reflections on Lake Michigan I
Florida
Gay Paree
Global Warning
Janet Jackson
Tweeting and Twittering
Highly Recommended
Alzheimer's
Holding On
Funeral
Visitation
Why?
February
To Emily Dickinson
Turning 70
Coffee Klatch
Sixteen
Her Voice
Grandest Moments

POEMS BY JOYCE SNOW

Organs
Bladder
Calendar Girl
Upgrades
Changing Face
Splitting Hairs
Salt & Pepper Arms
Old Friends Lost
Terrible Fight
Face in the Mirror
Classified Ad
Love and Marriage
Unfaithful Man
Blue Wine
College Reunion
Single at 70
Fugitive
Football Mom
His Other Lover
Writer's Excuses
Holidays
A Mother's Lament
Reflections on Lake
  Michigan II
Isabelle Puck
Guessing Game
Elder Cinderella
Letter to a Friend
Tom
The Letter
Grandpa's Knee
Old Lady
Life's Path

Chris and Joyce do readings for groups large or small. For available dates, contact them by

- **phone: 269.629.9553,**
- **email: laughsandwrinkles@gmail.com,**
- **U.S. mail: C&J Lines,**
  465 Gull Lake Drive,
  Richland, Michigan 49083

To order additional copies of *Laugh Lines and Other Wrinkles*, please send check or money order made payable to

C&J Lines
465 Gull Lake Drive
Richland, MI 49083

Single copies are $14.95, plus $3.00 shipping and handling. Michigan residents, please add 6% sales tax.

For information on quantity orders, contact us at laughsandwrinkles@gmail.com.